more titles in

The Secret Games of Maximus Todd!

Hyper to the Max
Clever Max invents a game to keep his Super Fidgets at bay for the day.

Frantic Friend Countdown
Everyone's got a best friend except him. But when a new kid arrives at the school, Max plays a secret game to make him Max's buddy.

Big Game Jitters
It's the soccer championship and Max's team is playing the school bully's team. As soon as the match starts, Max's gets a case of the Super Fidgets.

Flu Shot Fidgets
Max is at the doctor's office, when he invents a secret game to calm his Super Fidgets.

Camping Chaos
A wasp sting sets off a bad case of the Super Fidgets. Quick-thinking Max invents a game to keep them at bay.

School Trip

by L. M. Nicodemo

illustrated by Graham Ross

squirmies

Formac Publishing Company Limited
Halifax

Formac Publishing Company Limited recognizes the support of the Province
of Nova Scotia through Film and Creative Industries Nova Scotia. We are
pleased to work in partnership with the Province of Nova Scotia to develop
and promote our creative industries for the benefit of all Nova Scotians. We
acknowledge the support of the Canada Council for the Arts which last year
invested $157 million to bring the arts to Canadians throughout the country.

Cover design: Tyler Cleroux
Cover image: Graham Ross

Library and Archives Canada Cataloguing in Publication

Title: School trip squirmies / L.M. Nicodemo ; illustrated by Graham Ross.
Names: Nicodemo, L. M. (Linda M.), author. | Ross, Graham, 1962- illustrator.
Series: Nicodemo, L. M. (Linda M.). Secret games of Maximus Todd.
Description: Series statement: The secret games of Maximus Todd
Identifiers: Canadiana 2020027600X | ISBN 9781459505872 (hardcover) | ISBN
9781459505889 (softcover)
Classification: LCC PS8627.I245 S36 2021 | DDC jC813/.6—dc23

Formac Publishing Company Limited   Distributed in the United States by:
5502 Atlantic Street   Lerner Publishing Group
Halifax, Nova Scotia, Canada   241 1st Ave N
B3H 1G4   Minneapolis, MN, USA
www.formac.ca   55401

Printed and bound in Canada.
Manufactured by Friesens in Altona, MB in January 2021.
Job #272135

Contents

To Antonietta and Walter,
who provided a home filled
with love, laughter and lots of
books.

ACKNOWLEDGEMENTS

Sincerest gratitude goes to
Nicole Markotić, author and
teacher, who continually
challenges my work and through
wisdom, persistence and humour,
draws out the writer within.
I remain ever indebted.

Chapter One

All Aboard

GURGLE, GURGLE.

Max's stomach bubbled with excitement like a can of soda all shook up. Today Rosewood Elementary's grade three and four classes were going on

1

a field trip. To the city art gallery!

Everyone gathered in the school parking lot waiting to board a shiny orange school bus.

"ATTENTION!" Principal Hagglefinster clapped her hands. "When you hear

your name called, come up to
get your seat number from Mr.
Shep." The grade four teacher
waved a paper.

Assigned seating? Kids
groaned. Max hoped he'd get a
spot by the window.

"You'll be sitting with
a partner," the principal

continued. "Stick to her or him for the entire trip."

NO PROBLEMO,
THOUGHT MAX.

I'll be glue and tape rolled into one. Gl-ape.

"And please pick up your T-shirt. The colour tells you your group."

Max's teacher, Ms. Rudy, held up the shirts. Yellow, blue, purple, green and pink. They had the school's name and lion mascot printed on the back.

OOH, i WANT GREEN,

Max wished, crossing his fingers for good luck.

While the principal recited student names, Max rocked back and forth on his heels, trying to pay attention.

I hope I'm with Shiv, he thought. It'd be the best trip

ever if he and his best friend
belonged to the same group.
Max wriggled his feet from
within his sneakers and crossed
his toes. There was no such
thing as too much good luck.

"Todd, Maximus?" Ms.
Hagglefinster finally announced.

"WOOHOO!
THaT's me!"

Max shouted. Too loud. He
covered his mouth with his
hand "Oops . . . sorry," and
hopped over.

"You get purple," Ms. Rudy
said, handing Max a T-shirt. "My
favourite colour."

Max squinched his eyebrows. "Mine's green." **BUMMER.**

Mr. Shep scanned his clipboard. "Row eight, on the right side, with the other purples. Just look for Mandy Beth Bokely. You're sitting behind her."

Max groaned. Not #1 pest

Mandy Beth! She was the lint in his belly button. The broccoli in his stir-fry. The itch he couldn't reach to scratch. Now she'd be tagging along in his group for the entire field trip. Double bummer.

Grabbing the metal railing,

Max climbed onto the bus.
Sounds of chattering echoed
in his ears. Max waved to the
bus driver, who tipped his cap.
Then he edged down the aisle
counting out the rows.

One, Two, Three . . .

"Hey, Max," Mandy Beth
called as he approached. "We're
in the same group!"

"SEVEN," Max said loudly,
pretending not to hear. "EIGHT."

He stopped.

Spencer Vilane? Partnered
with the meanest, toughest,
bully-est fourth grader ever?!?
With one look,

He'd make a kid's heart pound, **THUMP THUMP**, and his knees knock, **PLONK PLONK**.

Spencer had his nose pressed against the bus window and was dragging it around, making sticky smudges. "Hmph!

Maximus Toad," he muttered.
"BETTER NOT BUG ME, OR ELSE!"

Max rolled his eyes. "Hmph! Hmph!" he imitated back, plopping down on the seat. He was not going to let Spencer bully him. Besides, what did OR ELSE mean anyway?

Chapter Two

The Wheels on the
Bus Go Round

Kids settled in. The teachers
did a head count. And then,
Ms. Rudy made a surprise
announcement. "If you all
behave today, you can sit with
whomever you choose on the
return trip."

Everyone cheered.

"YOU ROCK, MS. RUDY!"

someone shouted. Max
signalled Shiv who was three
rows back in the pink group.
His best buddy gave him a
thumbs-up.

Then the bus revved its engine and took to the road.

From the seat in front, Mandy Beth turned around. "Hey, let's play I Spy," she said.

Max frowned. "I can't, Mangy Breath. I'm very busy."

"Doing what?"

"Ignoring you," Max answered. **"AND iT'S a FULL-TiMe JOB."**

Spencer grunted. "Good one, nerd." Then he plugged in his earphones and turned back to the window.

Max leaned against his seat and closed his eyes. Though

the field trip had a rotten
start, it just had to get better.
Right? Once they got to the
gallery, he'd see paintings and
sculptures, and have a fancy
lunch in the cafeteria. Then
he'd ride back with Shiv.

Surely his luck was on the
upswing.

All at once, Max's feet

began to tingle, and his tummy to tickle and his arms to twinge. He suddenly felt like an overfilled water balloon — ready to bust.

It couldn't be. Could it? The great roar of a train racing down a track suddenly sounded in his head.

OH NO! IT IS! Max panicked. MY SUPER FIDGETS!

Now and again Max got so hyper, he could not keep still, could not think straight.

AND IT USUALLY — NO, ALWAYS — LED TO TROUBLE.

"What's with you?" Spencer sneered. "You got ants in your pants?"

Max wiggled in his seat. "Um, I gotta go."

He shuffled hurriedly down the aisle toward Ms. Rudy who sat at the front of the bus. He didn't need a washroom. He just

needed to move. Really bad.

I gotta come up with a secret game. Something to keep me busy on the inside so I won't be so fidgety on the outside!

"Can I help you, Max?" Ms. Rudy asked. "You shouldn't be standing up while the bus is moving."

Max's cheeks flushed.

"UM . . . WELL . . . UH . . . HOW MUCH LONGER UNTIL WE GET THERE?"

His teacher checked her watch. "Thirty minutes. Now go sit down, please."

THiRTY MiNUTES!

No way could he last that long.
Not without a game.

Max's mind whirred like
the blades of a helicopter
as he twisted to head back.
Unfortunately, his T-shirt caught
in the braid of a grade four girl.
"Ow!" she cried out.

"Sorry," he muttered,
tugging. *Darn my purple shirt!*
The purple shirt that should
have been green . . . **GREEN?!?**
That's it!

Max suddenly grinned. He
had his game. *From this point*
on, I'm all about green. I'll talk
green. I'll walk green. There'll

be no other colour for me.

And if he lost? If he didn't keep up with being green?

Max decided he would force himself to sit with Spencer on the bus ride home. Ugh. Spending the entire day with Spencer Vilane was worse than changing his baby sister's diapers. Even the poopy ones.

Chapter Three

it's Not Easy Being Green

Max eased down the aisle on high alert. He had to watch out for his favourite colour. And he spotted it everywhere!

In the green group that he passed.

"You're green. You're green.

You're green," he murmured
under his breath, his finger
sneaking to point at each kid
wearing a green T-shirt.

Someone's earrings. **"GReen."**

Another's sneakers. **"GReen."**

Back at his seat, Max glanced beyond Spencer to the outside scenery rolling by.

"Green," he mumbled, pointing at a passing cornfield. And, as the bus approached the edge of the city, he eyed two cars and a van. Green, green, green.

One thing was for sure, he was so busy looking out for green,

THeRe was no Time FOR HiS SUPeR FiDGeTS TO KiCK in.

"Hey, freak, enough staring out my window." Spencer

glared at him, removing an
earbud. "You're cramming my
personal space."

"Oh yeah? Well . . ." Max
meant to say something clever,
but then he looked at Spencer.

"Green eyes," he muttered.

"WHAT!?!" SHRieKeD SPeNceR. "YOU MUTANT! STOP LOOKiNG AT Me!"

Red faced, Max quickly glanced away. He noticed Mandy Beth's ponytail bobbing above her seat. There was a green elastic holding it in place. Very slowly, he lifted his hand and touched the band with a finger. "Green," he whispered.

SPONKiTY-CLONK.

Just then the bus drove over a pothole, making his finger

knock against Mandy Beth's
head. Yuck! Max quickly
snatched back his hand.

Too late. Mandy Beth spun
around. "Change your mind?
Wanna play now?"

Max was about to tell Mandy

Beth to go kiss a frog, a very GREEN one. Preferably with warts. But then he remembered that he had to keep control of his fidgets. "Yep. I'll play."

She clicked her tongue and grinned. "Good. You go first."

Settling back, Max searched around the bus.

"ALL RIGHT," He said. "i SPY WiTH MY LiTTLe eYe, SOMeTHiNG THAT iS . . . GREeN."

Chapter Four

Sticking to Spencer

Max trailed after Mandy Beth, down the bus steps and onto the art gallery parking lot.

NOT because she's the leader, he told himself.

Spencer pushed from behind. **"HURRY UP, TOAD."**

"Yeah!" Mandy Beth grinned. "Ms. Rudy's our chaperone!"

Max beamed. With his teacher in charge, Spencer wouldn't dare bully him. "Quit shoving," Max said, narrowing his eyes to shoot out invisible laser beams. **"OR ELSE!"**

"Gather round, purple people." Ms. Rudy carried a grape-coloured flag taped on the end of a metre stick. "First stop: Sculpture Gardens. Stay with your partners and follow me."

The Super Fidgets roiled under Max's skin as he stomped on the gravel. Crunch-crackle.

He hoped there'd be plenty of green in the gardens to use up his energy.

Ms. Rudy stopped at a tall iron gate. "Find your favourite work of art," she said, swinging it open.

Pebble paths ran in every

direction. Kids scattered among the sculptures. Max jogged to keep up with Spencer.

"Look," Spencer yelled, pointing at a giant copper octopus with long tentacles.

MAX WAVED HIS ARMS UP AND DOWN LIKE THE SEA CREATURE. "OOH. MY FAVOURITE."

Spencer raised a fist. "Mine! I saw it first." Then he took off around a corner.

Following, Max nearly slammed into a rock monster! "Aaah!" he screamed. Pebble claws grew out of a huge boulder. A mouth of jagged stones seemed to growl at them.

"Green," whispered Max, pointing at a pebble tooth.

"My favourite," Spencer declared.

"I'll take the octopus then," said Max.

Spencer stuck out his chin.

"THAT'S MY FAVOURITE TOO. FiND YOUR OWN."

No fair, thought Max. *Besides, how do I pick when Spencer gets to everything first?*

Spencer darted off again. Max dashed past a clump of

shrubs. **GREEN ... GREEN ... GREEN,**" he panted, spotting bushes shaped as a duck, a giant heart and a stegosaurus.

"Woohoo! Another favourite," called Spencer, approaching a throne made of car tires. **TAKE A SEAT,** read a sign. Spencer climbed up. "I am

the king of the gallery," he
announced. "Court Jester," he
said to Max. **"TeLL me a joKe."**

Max scratched his hair. "Um,
what's green and smells like
blue paint?"

"I dunno," said Spencer.

"Green paint!" chuckled Max.

Spencer cringed. "You're
fired." He bounced down and
then scurried off. No chance
for Max to try the throne. He
wished for a magic wand. To
zap Spencer's legs into cement.

Spencer led Max to a tilting
tower made of varnished pizza
boxes. Max slanted his body to
match. "Hey, it's the famous

Leaning Tower of Pizza!" he joked.

"Ha ha!" Spencer guffawed. "You're rehired! . . . And by the way, that statue is my favourite too!"

STATUE HOG,
MAX THOUGHT.

Just beyond the trees, he
spied a wire mesh sculpture
of an armadillo. *I'm beating
Spencer this time*, Max vowed,
pushing off with his sneakers.
But suddenly Spencer shouted,
"The purple flag's waving."
His teacher's signal to gather.
Bummer times ten!

While leaving the gardens,
Ms. Rudy asked Max which
work of art he liked best.
Max shrugged gloomily. "The
shrubs."

Chapter Five

Pipe Cleaner Picasso

Ms. Rudy led the kids through the gallery entrance to a room of windows. In front of a table with craft supplies stood a lady wearing a blue smock.

"Hello, students. I'm Cara. I work here at Riverside Gallery."

Green, thought Max, noticing a rainbow poster on the wall.

"Today, you'll create a sculpture," she continued. "Take five pipe cleaners and ten stringing beads. Create any shape you want." She pointed

to a pipe cleaner figure skipping
jump rope as an example.

Max noticed some beads.
"Green," he quietly said.

He decided to make a flock
of colourful birds. "I'll take an
orange pipe cleaner, please," he

asked Cara. "And a pink. And a red —"

BUT THEN HE SPOTTED THE GREEN ones!

OH no! His Game!

If he didn't stick to green he'd be sticking to Spencer. For the entire ride back.

"Um, I changed my mind," Max told her.

Back at his work station, he set down his materials. Five green pipe cleaners. Ten green beads. Boring!

All around him kids were busy shaping their sculptures. Spencer hunched over his

work. "I'm building an octopus attacking a shark," he said.

"ARE YOU MAKING a . . . a . . . GARBAGE CAN?"

Max thought fast. "A turtle." Bending and coiling the pipe cleaners, looping in the beads,

Max tried to form the shell.

"I like your broccoli statue," the lady from the art gallery said as she walked past.

Max pouted.

"iT's a TURTLe."

"Oh . . . yes, I see that now."
She smiled. "Would you like to
trade a green bead for another
colour, to highlight the eyes?"

"No thanks," said Max. He
puckered his brow. His statue
DID look like broccoli. *I'll hide
it in my pocket when I'm done.*

Ms. Rudy raised her hand.
"Exciting news, purples! The art
gallery wants to display your
sculptures at the
main enTrance!"

Cara passed out little cards.
"Please print your names on

the labels so every visitor will
know your fabulous work."

Though Max felt tempted to
sign "Mandy Beth" to his card,
he printed his initials instead,
very, very small. *Hope there
are a zillion other MT's out
there*, he silently wished.

Chapter Six

Salad
Woes

LUNCHTIME!

Kids crowded through the cafeteria doors.

"Good thing we get to sit with anybody we want," Max told Shiv as they stood at the counter to get their food.

Mandy Beth poked her head over Shiv's shoulder. "You can say that again!"

Max grimaced. *Well, ALMOST anybody we want.*

"Mmmm. Pizza."

Mandy Beth smacked her lips as she took a slice and placed it on her tray.

Shiv asked for two slices. "All this art makes me hungry."

Crispy crust. Stringy cheese. Spicy tomato sauce. What a meal!

Just as he was going to ask the server for a couple of slices, Max caught a glimpse of green behind the glass display. "What's that?"

"Spinach salad," she said.

VERY GREEN SPINACH SALAD.

Max liked salad. Back home, Granpops added apple chunks, walnuts and shredded cheddar.

But to Max, the spinach looked like a tree had **BaRFeD UP** its leaves into a bowl. His chest heaved. "I'll have that, please."

"Healthy choice, young man," said the server, passing the salad to Max.

The line edged forward toward the desserts.

"Aah. Strawberry pudding," sighed Mandy Beth.

Shiv reached for a brownie.

I gotta play my game, thought Max, grabbing a fruit cup. The greenest one. Pieces of kiwi and melon mixed with a few green grapes. Perfect.

In the double-door fridge,
Max chose lime punch. At *least
my green drink's kind of fun.*

They all sat down at a table
by the window.

"WHAT'S WITH YOUR LUNCH, MAX?"

Shiv asked, between chews.
"No pizza?"

"Didn't feel like it," he

answered, popping a grape into his mouth.

"But the brownies!" added Shiv. "Look! Sprinkles."

"I know." Max nodded. "I wanted to try something different."

"Yeah," said Mandy Beth, leaning over Max's tray. "Your lunch looks very healthy . . . and very green!" She sniffed loudly.

"i smell a game."

Darn that Mandy Beth! Max's forehead burned.

Usually Max kept his fidgets to himself even though Shiv

and Mandy Beth both knew.
He sometimes hated how his
hyper-ness made him feel
different than everyone else.
But now he was caught.

"Yep," he confessed. "My

Super Fidgets attacked on
the bus. I gotta do everything
green."

Mandy Beth nodded. "Like
your broccoli sculpture?"

Shiv stayed cheerful. "An
easy win, buddy. Lots of green
here. What could go wrong?"

YEAH. WHAT COULD POSSIBLY GO WRONG?

thought Max, wedging salad
into his mouth. Blech!

He roughly wiped his lips.

"IT WAS A TURTLE, MANDY BETH!"

Chapter Seven

And the
Answer is . . .

After lunch, Max's group entered a small theatre for a short movie about art. Kids sat on two wood benches facing a stage.

"Welcome." A man in a bow tie spoke beneath a spotlight.

"My name is Raffi. Hope you are enjoying our gallery."

Max criss-crossed his feet and then uncrossed them. He twiddled his thumbs. He exercised his eyebrows. **UP. DOWN. UP. DOWN.**

Sandwiched between Spencer and Mandy Beth, his fidgets itched to get out.

Max swivelled his head. No green to be seen! Anywhere.

"Before you watch the film, I have some prizes to hand out," said the man.

PRIZES?
MAX'S EARS PERKED.

"I'll ask each of you an art question. Get it right and you receive a coupon for a free ice cream."

Raffi asked the first student in the front row, "Please name

a material an artist can carve."

"Soapstone," she answered.

"Wonderful," praised Raffi,
and he handed her a pink
ticket.

EVERYONE CLAPPED.

The man from the gallery
moved to the next kid on the
bench. *He's going in order. I'll
be second last,* Max reasoned.

He just had to sit still until Raffi reached him.

If only he could spy something green. The floor? Nope. The walls? Uh uh. Spencer's hair? Max stifled a snort. Too bad.

Finally, Raffi made it to Spencer. "Can you name a tool that an artist uses?"

"A paintbrush and a pencil," Spencer blurted. "Can I get two coupons?"

The man grinned. "Sorry. One per person."

MY TURN. Max straightened his back and clasped his hands on his lap.

"Well, aren't you attentive? I sense a winner," chuckled Raffi. "Here's your question. Colour has meaning in art. It also holds meaning in life. Which colour of a traffic light means caution?"

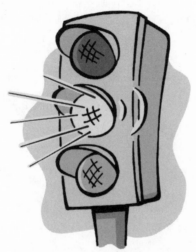

"Yel —" Max suddenly clamped his lips. He knew the

answer. But traffic lights had
three colours.

AND ONE
SUPER IMPORTANT
all-about-His-Game COLOUR
ROSE aBove THe OTHeRS.

The gallery man repeated his
question. A kid from the row
in front spun around to stare.

Sweat broke out on Max's forehead.

Do I answer to win an ice cream?

Lose my Game?

"Green," Max replied in a low voice.

"That's ri —" Raffi shook his head. The bow tie jittered. Kids sitting close enough to hear snickered. "Sorry. That's

incorrect," he said. "Let's try again. Which colour of a traffic light means stop?"

The question sounded loud in the small room's silence.

Max heard Mandy Beth giggle.

He dropped his chin to his chest and said again, "Green."

THE THEATRE ERUPTED in LAUGHTER.

Confused, the gallery man explained they were running out of time, and he moved on to Mandy Beth.

"Wow," whispered Spencer.

"Even my goldfish would have got that one right."

Once the lights dimmed and the film played, Max let a few tears fall. *What could go wrong?* Shiv had asked. Max knew that answer.

LOTS.

Chapter Eight

Feeling Blue

Down the gallery's hallways, Max trudged after Spencer. Colourful art hung on the walls. Velvet ropes protected a painting of rocks and trees on a shoreline. "This one's famous," said Spencer.

Max didn't care. His
excitement had vanished.
POOF. He could not forget the
fiasco in the theatre.

Mostly because his pesky
partner kept reminding him.

At a watercolour of a
butterfly, Spencer said,
"Butterflies are free like my ice
cream."

Green bushes, thought Max.

When they stood at an oil
painting of outdoor skaters,
Spencer commented,

**"BET THEY'RE COLD . . .
LiKE iCE CREAM."**

"Green," muttered Max, noticing an ice skater's pea-coloured cap.

Spencer shook his finger at a drawing of city buildings. "Done in pencil. One of my RIGHT answers. I had two," he bragged.

"HOW many DiD YOU Have, Max?"

Max slumped his shoulders, wishing he could go home.

Chapter Nine

UN-
Green

Though he didn't feel like
it, Max followed Cara, the
sculpture lady, as she sketched
a cat. Learning to draw with
charcoal was the last activity
of the day.

"Charcoal's loads of fun,"

she said keenly. Her fingers rubbed the dark lines. They turned to furry blurs. "And so easy to alter . . ." Cara wiped her page with white putty and the cat's whiskers disappeared like magic! The kids in Max's group oohed and aahed.

Cara laughed. "Your turn now."

Max stood at his table holding a stick of charcoal. His drawing paper lay blank.

"DOES CHARCOAL COME IN GREEN?" HE ASKED.

The gallery lady shook her head. "No other colour.

Charcoal is about shade and tone."

But I'm about green! A worry bubble churned in Max's stomach. How can I make green art with an UN-green piece of charcoal?

"Hey, do you like my picture?" Spencer asked slyly from the table next to Max's.

Max glanced over. A triple scoop ice cream? **REALLY?**

He recalled all the trouble
he'd had with green, and he
felt his eyes water.

Clenching the charcoal, Max
drew a tall traffic light. Then
he connected his broccoli-turtle
sculpture to the side and pizza
tower below that. What a
mess! *I'm gonna lose my game!*
Frustrated, Max moved to
crumple his page.

Instead he stood back and
looked again. The drawings
seemed to make the letter R.

BaH-DiNG!

An iDea BURST SUDDenLy in MaX'S HeaD.

Was it possible?

Inspired, Max drew shrubs on the other side of the R. They formed the letter G.

Slices of kiwi, chunks of melon and the can of lime punch made an E.

He chuckled.

YES! IT WAS POSSIBLE.

"Whatcha laughing at, nerd?" Spencer scowled.

"You got a crumb on your nose," Max said.

Spencer scratched at his face, leaving a charcoal smear.

"Higher," Max told him, and Spencer rubbed closer to his

eyebrow. Another dark streak.

"GOT iT!"

Max stifled a giggle and happily went back to designing another E.

The art room door creaked

open. Raffi, from the theatre, sauntered in. "I've got a spare ice cream coupon to give for my favourite work of art."

No chance I'll win, thought Max. But somehow, it didn't bother him. He had survived his Super Fidgets and Spencer and his game. Forget the ice cream.

i DeSeRVe a TROPHY! He muSeD.

Once Raffi made his rounds, Cara announced, "We're out of time! Please hold up your art for us all to admire." Luckily Max had just finished his last letter: N.

Raffi twirled the pink ticket. "You've done an amazing job. I wish I had more coupons."

"No probs. We all already have one," Spencer said loudly. He hitched his thumb at Max. "Except him." The other students hooted. Max ducked behind his page.

"Well, what a coincidence," Raffi continued. "This young man's artwork happens to be my favourite!"

What? Max peeked over his drawing. *He's just saying that because he feels sorry for me!*

"And I'm not just saying that because I feel sorry," said Raffi,

taking hold of Max's picture. "Charcoal is about shade and tone. Not colour."

So I've heard, thought Max.

Raffi turned around, urging all the students to look. "But this fine lad managed to express green without using the colour green. In fact," Raffi said, smiling at Max,

"everything about your charcoal drawing says green . . . lit-er-al-ly. well done!"

Spencer's jaw dropped. A couple of kids clapped. And then the whole room exploded with applause.

Chapter Ten

Too Much of a Green Thing

"Which flavour are you going to get?" Shiv asked Max. They were leaning over the art gallery's glass display of ice cream cartons.

Ms. Rudy allowed everyone to have their free treat before

boarding the bus home. A perfect ending to a sort of, somewhat perfect field trip.

"You can have the window seat on the ride back," Shiv offered. "It's been a rough day."

Max smiled at his best
friend. "We'll take turns."
He passed his coupon to the
ice-cream server. "Chocolate
Caramel Tornado, please . . . in
a waffle cone."

"AREN'T YOU FORGETTING SOMETHING?"

From behind, Mandy Beth's high-pitched voice grated in Max's ear.

"Like your annoying face?"
Max replied. "I'm trying."

"How about Mint Chocolate
Chip?" she suggested, taking
a slurp from her cone. A
smear of candy-cane ice cream
stained her cheek.

Max winced. "No way! Smells
like toothpaste."

"You might like it, Max,"
Mandy Beth insisted. She
pressed her napkin against her
lips to stifle a laugh.

"AFTER ALL, IT'S SUCH a LOVELY COLOUR."

Max flicked his eyelids and gasped. Curse that Mandy Beth!

He rushed to the side of the counter just as the server bent over the carton, scoop in hand. "Sir! Can I change my order?" he called, waving his arms to get the worker's attention.

"I SUDDENLY HAVE a CRAVING . . . FOR SOMETHING . . . GREEN."